To Val and Julie,

I hope you enjoy my book
and find a new friend in Boots.
Enjoy!

Best Wishes,

Carol, Steven and Boots

Boots

Boots Finds a New Home

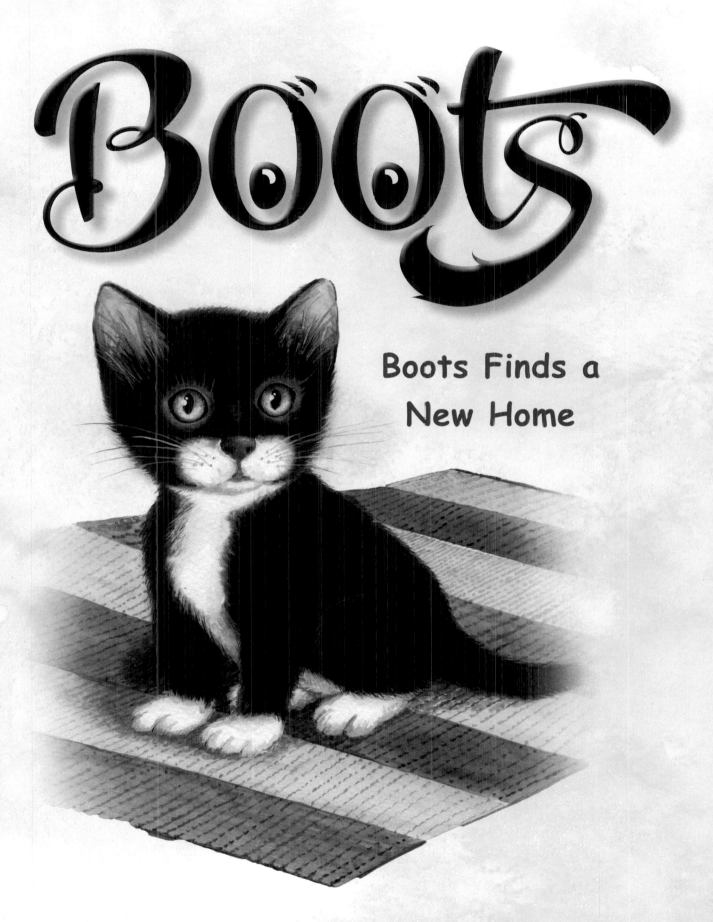

WRITTEN BY CAROL S. HERVIN

Illustrated by Doina Cociuba

Book Publishers Network

P. O. Box 2256

Bothell, WA 98041

425-483-3040

www.bookpublishersnetwork.com

10 9 8 7 6 5 4 3 2 1

LCCN: 2011909826

ISBN 13: 978-1-935359-87-6

ISBN 10: 1-935359-87-8

CPSIA facility code: BP 313019

Dedication

♡

This book is dedicated to Jeff,

my wonderful husband.

Thank you for your never-ending

support, encouragement,

belief in me and my project,

and for loving

Boots as much as I do!

One warm and sunny day, when I was a tiny baby kitten, I was left all by myself in a large grassy field. I am not sure why I was there all by myself, but after a while, I began to feel alone and afraid.

The field seemed huge and endless with green scratchy grass so tall I could not see over it. I felt lost. I began to cry with sad little meows.

Have you ever felt alone or afraid? What did you do? Did someone come and comfort you and help you?

After a while, a young girl walked by, saw me and picked me up. As soon as she picked me up, I felt safe and protected. She began to talk to me. The girl had a very kind voice and a beautiful smile. To me she was an angel. I was no longer alone or afraid.

She carried me to her house, and that was the beginning of happy changes for me. I did not know what was going to happen next. I just knew I did not feel alone anymore. Would I live with this girl at her house? Would this be my new home now? I did not know. I was very curious.

5

As it turned out, this would not be my new home because the girl had allergies to cats. Imagine that, being allergic to me! I was not allergic to her, I did not really understand this. But what she did next for me was the best gift ever. She found a family for me the next day, and they took me to their house. My life was about to change in a most wonderful way.

Have you ever been given a very special gift that made you very happy? What was it?

The people in my new family are very nice. I felt very comfortable with them right away. They are a woman we call Mom, a man we call Dad, a boy we call Bud, and a girl we call Peaches.

Peaches is away at college, and I do not get to see her very often, but when she comes home to visit, she always looks for me and holds me. I am really liking all of the attention they give me. The boy we call Bud even lets me sleep on his soft, comfortable bed. I feel so special!

I loved my new home and family from the start. I can tell that my family loves me too. I am always being carefully held and carried around and talked to so nicely. I feel safe and happy and sleep soundly most of the day, as kittens do.

My new home seems very large and has so many rooms that I often feel lost until I hear a voice from my family looking for me. "Boots," – they will call, "where are you?" I will run as fast as I can to find them. They smile and pick me up, and I purr with happiness.

There are stairs in my new home. I was afraid of them at first. They seemed like giant mountains to climb and so hard for me. I would very slowly work my way to the top, one stair at a time. When I turned around to look down, it made me feel dizzy. By the time I finally reached the top, I needed a nap!

Does climbing up stairs make you feel tired too?

13

14

My favorite room in my new home is the family room. I like this room the best because this is where my family seems to spend the most time, and I am always together with them, sleeping on their lap. Being together with my family is the happiest thing for me.

Do you have a favorite room in your house? What is it? Why is this your favorite room?

I have fun toys to play with at my new home! I have a little fuzzy gray mouse that squeaks, a tiny purple horse, and three soft little balls. My favorite toy is the little gray mouse that squeaks. It is my favorite because I can hold the end of it in my mouth and carry it around the house.

I like having toys to play with. My family seems to like to play with my toys too. They will toss my little toys up in the air and watch me as I run to catch them. I do not understand this game, but it always makes them laugh. I like to have fun with my family.

Do you have toys too?

What is your favorite toy?

17

18

I have not told you how I got my name, have I? Well, when you look at my picture, can you guess how I got my name? Yes, it is because I have four all-white feet! My family thought my feet looked like little boots, so they named me Boots.

What is your name? Did your family give you your name because of how your feet look too? I like my name. Do you like your name too?

I am very happy and thankful for my new home and my new family and thankful that I was found in the field on that sunny warm day by the angel girl. Is there something you are thankful for? What is it?

I am going to take another little cat-nap now. Telling you my story was fun for me, but it made me a little tired too. We kittens require a lot of napping.

I like naps. Do you take naps too?

Good-bye for now my friend.

I have more to tell you when I see you in my next story...

Love, Boots

21

Carol and Boots live in Seattle, Washington, where the air is clean, the hills are green, and cats (and other critters) are welcome friends.

After receiving a Telly Award for Outstanding Achievement in film production, Carol was encouraged to direct her creative interests to writing. Her wish is that you truly enjoy it and also discover a new friend in Boots!